BRASSY
THE FIRE ENGINE
Saves the City

by DENNIS SMITH   Illustrated by JUSTIN MILLER

LB
L   Y
New York ·· Boston

For the little ones in my everyday life:
Fiona and Julia,
and
Fayre, Henry, and Carlin
Love you every one. . . .
—D.S.

To my grandparents Lillian Jones and
Donald and Beulah Miller for their
unwavering belief in me.
—J.M.

Little, Brown and Company

Time Warner Book Group
1271 Avenue of the Americas, New York, NY 10020
Visit our Web site at www.lb-kids.com

First Edition: October 2005
Based on *The Little Fire Engine That Saved the City*, by Dennis Smith, published in 1990 by Doubleday.

Library of Congress Cataloging-in-Publication Data

Smith, Dennis, 1940-
    Brassy the fire engine saves the city / by Dennis Smith ; illustrated by Justin Miller.— 1st ed.
        p. cm.
    Summary: Brassy the fire engine is the only truck small enough to reach an out-of-control fire, and he and his friend Captain Bill save the city.
    ISBN 0-316-76135-4
    [1. Fire engines—Fiction 2. Fire extinction—Fiction.] I. Miller, Justin, 1978- ill. II. Title.
PZ7.S644714Br 2005
[E]—dc22

2004004712

10 9 8 7 6 5 4 3 2 1

Book design by Saho Fujii

PHX

Printed in China

The illustrations for this book were done in oil paint on Bristol Vellum paper.
The text was set in OldClaude, and the display type is Estro.

Captain Bill had been hoping for a new fire engine, and he was very pleased as he watched the Little Fire Engine back up into his firehouse for the very first time.

"He's not very big," Captain Bill said, "but he is bright and shining. Look at that big brass bell right up front."

"Hey," Firefighter Pat said, "let's call him Brassy."

"Yes," the Captain said. "He's strong and spiffy, and brassy too. We have a truly fine fire department now."

The other firefighters crowded around the new fire engine. One began to buff the big brass bell, and another sat behind the steering wheel and pressed on the air horn: *toot, toot, toot.*

"That's just three toots," Captain Bill said. "We need a fourth toot."

"Why?" Firefighter Pat asked.

"Because," the Captain answered, "Brassy needs a number, and we are giving him number four."

The firefighters then cheered. "Welcome to our firehouse, Brassy," they said.

"Yes," Captain Bill said, patting Brassy's fender, "this is your fire-house now, and you will serve our town well."

Brassy had found a home, and that made him so happy. He laughed as he tooted the fourth toot, and Captain Bill laughed along with him.

Firefighter Nancy began to paint a big golden "4" on each door, and Firefighter Pat clanged the big brass bell. Everyone was having a happy time.

But, life in the firehouse isn't all fun. Emergencies happen, and the firefighters have to help when they are needed. Every time there was a fire in town, the firefighters would race to the firehouse and put on their firefighting coats and helmets. Captain Bill would crank up Brassy's engine and drive him off to fight the fire.

There was much excitement as the firefighters pulled the long white hose through the streets, and as the fire chief shouted orders through a slender silver trumpet. Brassy would puff and grind to pump the water through the hoses and onto the fire.

After each fire, Captain Bill took Brassy back to the firehouse, and the fire-fighters gave him a good scrubbing down. Firefighter Pat and Firefighter Nancy would take extra-special care buffing and polishing Brassy's fenders, doors, and the big brass bell until the Little Fire Engine glistened.

"Now we are proud and ready," Captain Bill said, "for our next alarm."

And there were many alarms. People need help when a house or a store catches fire, like when Mr. Paulson's Hardware Store burned down. Captain Bill saved Mr. Paulson by putting a ladder up against the side of the store. And, when people get hurt by falling down, or when there is an accident on a street or a highway, Firefighter Pat and Firefighter Nancy are always ready to bandage an arm or a leg.

The firefighters also helped when there was a flood in Mr. Walker's basement, and when Mrs. Hanratty's cat, Jinx, climbed to the roof of Mrs. Hanratty's house and could not get down.

As the years passed, the town grew into a city, and the fire department responded to more and more alarms. Some firefighters were transferred to other firehouses as the fire department grew, and new firefighters came to work with Brassy in his firehouse. But Captain Bill did not transfer, and, with Firefighter Pat and Firefighter Nancy helping, he kept Brassy looking strong and ready. Whenever a fender got dented, or some paint was chipped off a door, Captain Bill was the first one to grab a hammer or a paintbrush to repair the Little Fire Engine.

Brassy and Captain Bill had become good friends, and Brassy always did his best to make his friend proud of him, to show him how much he cared about driving safely through the streets to the alarms, and pumping the water as fast as he could to put out the fires.

Then things began to
change, and Brassy noticed that
he was no longer placed right up front
to fight the flames. Instead, the fire chief kept him
off to the side, and put newer and bigger fire engines up front.

At one fire, Brassy was doing a very good job of spraying his
water onto the roof of a burning building, when suddenly a
bigger fire engine moved right up in front and blocked Brassy
from spraying any water at all.

Brassy was disappointed, but he did not let it show to the firefighters. He kept smiling, because he was still glad to be a part of
the fire department and to be Captain Bill's friend. And, also,
Brassy knew deep in his heart that he was as good a pumper
as any fire engine
ever made.

He continued to go to every alarm, and he always did the very best he could do. Then one day, Brassy saw that Captain Bill looked very sad. "The fire department is going to transfer you, Brassy," Captain Bill said. "They are sending you to another firehouse on the other side of town, where it will be slower, and where you can rest. You have done a very good job for the city, and you'll like your new firehouse."

But Brassy did not like his new firehouse at all. It was dark and dusty, and the firefighters did not shine him the way Firefighter Pat and Firefighter Nancy did. And he missed his friend Captain Bill.

Captain Bill missed Brassy, too, and asked the chief if he would bring Brassy back so that they could work together again.

"No," the chief said. "We need him on the other side of town."

Captain Bill was sad and kept asking the chief, again and again, to bring Brassy back.

But, the chief kept saying "No."

Then one day, there was a very big fire, the biggest that had ever occurred in the city. Many buildings were burning, and all the firefighters knew the fire was out of control.

"If we don't stop this fire soon," the chief said, "the whole city will burn down."

"We can stop it at Old Town Street," Captain Bill said.

"But," the Chief said, "that is the oldest street in the city, and it is so narrow. A fire truck is too wide to fit."

"I know one fire engine that will fit into that narrow street," Captain Bill answered. "Brassy—the Little Fire Engine."

"Yes," the chief said. "That might do it."

"I'll go get him," Captain Bill said.

Brassy had never been as happy as when Captain Bill cranked up his engine and drove to the fire. He kept clanging his bell and tooting his air horn until he reached Old Town Street.

"You are our only hope," the chief said when he saw Brassy. "Now get in there and put as much water as you can on those burning buildings."

There was not much room to get through the
narrow street, but Captain Bill and Brassy went forward
ever so slowly and deliberately as the firefighters cheered them on.
"You can do it, Brassy," Firefighter Nancy said.

Finally, they passed through Old Town Street, and Brassy was right there in the very front of the fire. He pumped and pumped as hard as he could, and the water sprayed out at the buildings, cooling them down, putting the flames out one window at a time.

"Good job, Brassy," the chief yelled, "good job. You are stopping the fire."

"And," Captain Bill added, "you're saving the city, too."

Brassy had never been so proud of Captain Bill and the Fire Department. He was proud of the Chief, too.

The next day, sitting in his old firehouse, the Little Fire Engine beamed as he heard
the Chief say, "We are transferring Brassy back to this firehouse, because we think that the Little Fire Engine and Captain Bill
should always work together."

"We do make a great team," Captain Bill said.

"Hooray," said Firefighter Pat and Firefighter Nancy.

And then an alarm came in, and they all went off to fight
another fire, and to help the people of the city.